THROW A KISS,

HARRY

New Edition

Story and pictures by **Mary Chalmers**

Harper & Row, Publishers

Library of Congress Cataloging-in-Publication Data
Chalmers, Mary, date
  Throw a kiss, Harry / story and pictures by Mary Chalmers.
    p.   cm.
  Summary: Wandering away from his mother, Harry the Cat gets stuck
in a tree until a fireman comes to his rescue.
    ISBN 0-06-021246-2 : $. — ISBN 0-06-021245-4 (lib. bdg.) :
$
  [1. Cats—Fiction.   2. Behavior—Fiction.]   I. Title.
PZ7.C354Th   1990   89-49064
[E]—dc20   CIP
                                                                   AC

to Boats

One morning
Harry went for a walk
with his mother.

He saw a turtle.

"Hello, turtle," said Harry.

"Harry, leave the turtle alone,"
said his mother.

"Come along," she said.

Mother stopped to talk to a friend.

Harry wandered off by himself.

He watched an ant.

He sniffed a flower.

10

He climbed up a tree, and . . .

jumped to the roof of a house.

It was very high.

"Harry!" cried his mother.

"Come down this instant!"

But Harry didn't know how.

"I'm scared!" cried Harry.

Mother called the fire department.

They sent their best

hook and ladder truck.

They put up a long, long ladder.

A fireman carried Harry safely down.

Harry liked that.

Mother gave Harry a big hug.
"See what happens when you go
wandering off by yourself?" she said.
"Now come along home."
But Harry did not want to go home.

He waved to the fireman.

The fireman waved back.

Harry waved again.

19

"Why don't you throw a kiss
to the fireman?" asked Harry's mother.
"No!" said Harry.

"Why not?" asked Mother.

21

"Because," said Harry.

"I think the fireman would like a kiss,"
said Mother.

"No, he wouldn't!" said Harry.

"Come on home then," said his mother.

But Harry stayed behind.

He slowly raised his paw...

and blew a kiss!